Production and copyright © 1992 Rainbow Grafics International—Baronian Books SC, Brussels, Belgium.
English translation text copyright © 1993 by Lothrop, Lee & Shepard Books.

First Edition   1   2   3   4   5   6   7   8   8   10

Library of Congress Cataloging in Publication data was not available in time for publication of this book, but can be obtained from the Library of Congress.   ISBN 0-688-12379-1   Library of Congress Catalog Card Number: 92-54429

The Tightrope Walker

Bernadette Gervais and Francisco Pittau

Lothrop, Lee & Shepard Books
New York

Phil had always dreamed of walking on a tightrope.

First he practiced on the edge of his bed.

Then he practiced on the clothesline.

One day a giant tightrope stretched before him.
"Look out!" mooed the cow.
"Be careful!" bleated the sheep.
But Phil was ready.

Soon he had left his village far behind.

The rope went on and on—

over the fields,

and through the sky,

all the way to Louise's house.

"My goodness!" said Louise. "How on earth
  did you get here?"
"I came through the sky," Phil told her. "I am
  a tightrope walker!"

Louise's cat, Fred, thought tightrope-walking
looked like fun.
"Don't wobble the rope," Phil warned him.

Phil and Fred tightrope-walked right through
the city...

to the edge of the sea...

and even further.

Once Fred lost his footing,

but Phil came to the rescue in the nick of time.

"Land ahead!" called Phil,

and into the mountains they marched.

"What funny-looking birds," said the bears.

In a little while, Phil and Fred came to a village,

and then to a familiar clothesline.

"We're home!" said Phil.

"Just in time for bed."